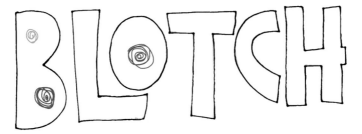

A Tale of Forgiveness and Grace

by Andy Addis

Illustrated by Tatio Viana

Nashville, Tennessee

Dedication

Blotch *is dedicated to my family, for their life and love.*
To my sons, Noah and Nathan, for their faith and awesomeness.
To my wife, Kathy, for her believing and nudging.
And, mostly, to my King, for taking away my blotches.

Illustrations © 2016 B&H Publishing Group

Published by B&H Publishing Group, Nashville, Tennessee

ISBN: 978-1-4336-8690-0

Dewey Decimal Classification: JF

Subject Heading: SIN–FICTION / SALVATION–FICTION /
REDEMPTION–FICTION

Scripture references taken from the Holman Christian Standard Bible (HCSB),
copyright © 1999, 2000, 2002, 2003, 2009 by Holman Bible Publishers.

All rights reserved. Printed in LongGang District, Shenzhen, China.

September 2016

2 3 4 5 6 7 8   20 19 18 17 16

Contents

A Letter to Parents

Blotch is a story to be read aloud and discussed with children. It is my hope that the story of Blotch will open conversations about God's goodness, our sinfulness, and the blessing of Jesus.

Because the aim of this book is guided discussion with children, here is its suggested use:

1. *Pray about the opportunity to discuss Christ with your children often.*

2. *Read the entire story yourself before reading it to your children.*

3. *Read the book aloud to your children one chapter per day, and use the discussion guide at the back for each chapter. Remember to read the guide and prepare ahead of time.*

4. *Be prepared to pray with your children about salvation, the assurance of salvation, or any other needs as he or she is ready. Don't force your child to make a decision or to wait for the end of the story to make one. Let the Father draw him or her as He pleases!*

Isaiah 1:18 tells us, "Though your sins are like scarlet, they will be as white as snow; though they are as red as crimson, they will be like wool." My hope is that *Blotch* will help young readers grasp that message: their sins *can* be forgiven, and they can find salvation in the one true King.

Thank you so much for caring for your children enough to share the most important thing you can: the love of Jesus!

Seeking more of Him and less of me,

Andy Addis

John 3:30

www.andyaddis.com

Chapter 1
The Journey Begins

Blotch was the smallest brother, in the smallest family, in the smallest village in the whole kingdom. As the bright orange sun began to set, little Blotch sat in the same place where he ended every day.

He was perched on the edge of a very small cliff on the edge of a very small pond looking into the clear and perfectly still water. The surface of the water was like a mirror, and Blotch would often stare at his reflection for hours.

It's not that he liked the way he looked. In fact, it was just the opposite. Blotch spent his evenings trying to race the vanishing light of the sun as he counted all the spots and stains upon his face and body. But every day as the light faded, his mother called him to dinner before he could get to the end of his counting. There were just too many stains.

Blotch was not born with all his stains—none of his people were. They all began their lives with only one small mark, but the number of stains grew and grew with each passing day. No matter how they tried, they could not keep from getting new stains. The stains were part of who they were.

With a name like Blotch, he thought about those stains and spots a lot. Of course, the stains were no mystery. Everyone knew where they came from.

If you told a lie, a stain appeared.

When you said something mean, there was another spot.

Disobeying parents? Oops, here comes another.

Whenever anyone was bad, mean, or just did something wrong, another stain would appear. Even the best people Blotch knew had their own stains!

He didn't know exactly what had caused each of their spots, but he knew it wasn't anything good.

Although no one liked the marks, no one knew how to make them go away.

But Blotch was a determined boy, and he was determined to find the answer.

As the sun faded behind the hills, Blotch made his way home. It was time for dinner, and he knew he would not solve the problem of the stains tonight.

Around the table with his father, mother, and two older brothers, Blotch sat quietly while they talked about their day. They shared stories of bullies at school, mean conversations at work, and rude people at the store. These were the kinds of things stained people talked about.

Blotch didn't say a word—that is, until his mother turned to him and said, "Well, my little Blotch, why so quiet tonight?"

Blotch looked up quickly, sending a single tear sliding down his cheek. "How do we get rid of the stains?" His voice was shaky but loud.

Every voice at the table went silent, and every eye focused on Blotch.

"I'm tired of the spots, the marks, and the stains. I want them to go away!" He didn't know whether to cry or be mad.

His oldest brother spoke first. "Oh, be quiet, Blotch. Everyone's got them." As he spoke, a faint little spot appeared just under his left eye.

Blotch's middle brother didn't say a word, but he didn't have to. When a stain appeared on the end of his brother's nose, Blotch knew he must be thinking mean things about him.

Just then, Blotch's father spoke up, "Now, now Blotch. Your brother is right. Unfortunately, stains are just a part of life. You need to learn to live with them like everybody else."

But Blotch didn't want to live with the stains. Deep down he believed they were not meant to have spots, and he was going to find some way, any way, to make them go away.

A little embarrassed, Blotch pushed away from the table and walked around to sit next to his father. Blotch whispered, "Dad, what if there is a way we can get rid of the spots?"

"Well, I suppose that would be wonderful, my little Blotch, but how in the world could that ever be? We have always had spots," said his father.

Blotch felt his stomach tighten. He had thought about his plan almost every night while sitting by the pond and counting stains, but saying it out loud would make it much more real. Blotch swallowed the lump in his throat and continued, "Dad, what if someone knows how to get rid of the stains? What if someone in one of the other villages knows what to do? What if the King of the kingdom could make them go away?"

Blotch sat up taller and wiped the tears from his eyes. He looked right at his father. Feeling bigger than he had ever felt, he asked one more question.

"Dad, I need to find an answer. Would you let me go on an adventure to see if someone knows how to get rid of the stains?"

Blotch's heart pounded like thunder as he waited

for his father's reply. It seemed like an hour before he heard the quiet answer: "Yes."

Blotch couldn't believe it. He looked up at his father and saw that this time the tears were in his father's eyes. Even though Blotch was young, his father knew he couldn't deny Blotch the chance to try to find the answers he was searching for.

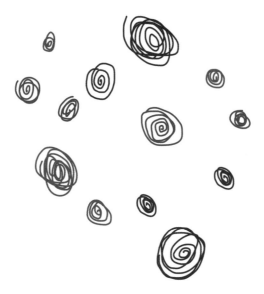

Chapter 2
The Hiders

Early the next morning, Blotch packed a backpack with a few sandwiches, a sleeping bag, and a map. He kissed his mother, hugged his father and brothers, and bravely set off down the road looking for his answer.

After an hour or so, he heard the sounds of a noisy, bustling village. Getting closer, he saw many people working, walking, and talking to one another. It was much like his village, but something was very different.

Blotch didn't see any stains!

As he looked around, he admired the rows of white picket fences and lush, green lawns. The streets were spotless, and every single person looked neat and polished.

Blotch was usually shy, but he couldn't help but stare. Seeing an entire village of people with no stains, no spots, no marks—he could hardly believe his eyes. *Could I have already found the answer to my question?* he thought to himself.

Blotch was so excited that he forgot his manners and ran up to the first group of strangers he saw. "You have no stains!" he exclaimed.

A smile stretched across the face of a tall stranger carrying a box full of bottles. The man responded in a very snooty voice, "Why, no, I do not! No one here in Hiderville has stains. We are simply better than those . . . those stained people."

Blotch was so amazed that he didn't really notice

17

the stranger's insult. Instead, he reached out to touch the arm of the stain-free man. The stranger's smile quickly disappeared as he jerked his arm away.

"I would thank you to mind your own business," he said before forcing a smile again.

Blotch stepped back and lowered his head. "Oh, I . . . I'm sorry."

He spent the rest of the morning walking around the village and trying not to stare at all the stain-less people. Blotch could tell they were also trying (although not as hard) to keep from staring at Blotch's stains from head to toe. And whenever he walked near a group of villagers, they would step far off the sidewalk to avoid him.

Blotch couldn't quite figure it out. These villagers may not have any marks or stains, but they certainly weren't very nice. After a while, Blotch got the courage to ask a few villagers how it was that they had no stains.

"None of your business."

"That's for me to know and you to find out."

"Why don't you go back where you came from?"

The harder Blotch tried to discover the secret of

Hiderville, the harder the villagers tried to hide the answer. But with every rude response, Blotch just grew more and more determined to find answers. He was so focused on his mission that he didn't hear the rumbles of thunder from the summer storm passing through. In fact, he never would have noticed if it were not for the way everyone in Hiderville began running for cover.

"Run, run!" came the cries of mothers to their children. Grown men pushed through the crowds of people, not caring who they shoved down on their way to get inside . . . somewhere, anywhere.

Blotch shouted to anyone who would listen, "It's just a little rain. Why are you all so afraid?"

Just then a booming clap of thunder announced the presence of a downpour. Everyone had made it inside. That is, everyone except Blotch and the tall stranger he had met when he first arrived. The man had dropped his box in the commotion and was frantically trying to pick up all the bottles.

In the rain, this tall stranger looked different. He looked sad—not sad like he got caught in the rain, but sad that something horrible had happened.

As the rain fell on the once spotless man, Blotch could see that the stranger now looked like him, stains and all.

The rain had washed away his secret. The people of this village were really no different from those in the town Blotch had come from. They had just as many stains; they had only covered them. And the rain revealed everything the people were hiding.

Blotch picked up his backpack, glanced at the sad, stained stranger, and walked away from Hiderville.

Chapter 3
The Pretenders

A few miles down the road, the rain had stopped, and Blotch's clothes began to dry. He was counting the stains on his arm when he came over the top of a hill. Down below, he saw a cheerful little place with several small houses and lots of people.

As he reached the village, he looked down the dirt road and saw neat, well-worn houses on each side. And everywhere he looked, he saw stained people like himself. That made Blotch feel much more at home, but he also realized that he wouldn't find his answers here. It was obvious that no one in this village knew how to get rid of the stains.

As the sun began to sink behind the hills, Blotch decided this would be a good place to spend the night. "Excuse me, sir," he said to one man. "I'm traveling from village to village on a search for answers. Do you know a place where I can stay tonight?"

"Well, of course, my little friend," said the kind man. "There's always room for one more around our campfire. You can join my family tonight." Blotch was relieved to find welcoming people, even if they did have as many stains as anyone he'd ever seen.

As Blotch walked with his new friend through the village, he saw a playground of stained children, a couple of smiling stained ladies putting out the laundry, and several stained men working in the streets. He arrived at his new friend's home just as the last of the sun disappeared behind the hills.

Blotch unrolled his sleeping bag next to a campfire. "Thank you for letting me stay with you," he told the man and his family. "You're the first friendly people I've met on my journey."

"We're glad you're here!" The man looked over the fire at Blotch. "I've lived in Pretendtown my whole life. I always look forward to meeting strangers who are passing through. Tell me, my friend, what are you looking for on your journey?"

Blotch wanted to tell his new friends, but he wasn't so sure how they would respond. Would they make fun of him as his brothers had? Would they jerk away like the Hiders?

Still, Blotch knew he wouldn't find any answers if he didn't have the courage to ask. "I . . . I'm on a journey to see if anyone knows how to get rid of all our stains," he explained.

There was an awkward pause. Troubled faces looked back at him from all around the campfire.

"Uh, stains? What is a stain?" asked the young boy sitting by his father.

Blotch didn't know how to respond. Could his new friends really not see all their stains? Confused, he quickly turned his focus to finding a sandwich in his backpack while the campfire crackled through the silence. The taste of the sandwich made him a bit homesick.

The family talked late into the evening. Each time Blotch tried to turn the conversation back toward the stains, his friends changed the subject.

Finally, when Blotch asked, the man answered, "Well, I guess we can talk about stains, but I don't see why they are so interesting to you. When we get stains on our clothes, we just take them down to the river and wash them." The man never looked up from the fire, poking a stick at the flames as he spoke.

"No," Blotch began, "I'm not talking about stains on our clothes. I'm talking about these stains we have all over our bodies." As Blotch spoke, he waved his arms around in the light of the campfire to show his stains.

The sister, who looked to be about Blotch's age, giggled at the odd behavior. Her father cleared his throat. "Look, Blotch," he began, "I don't have any stains, and you don't have any stains. There's no such thing as stains."

Blotch was speechless. How could he see the spots so easily and his new friend not see a thing?

Blotch set his sandwich on top of his backpack, walked around the fire to the man and his daughter, and sat between them. He rolled up his sleeve and started pointing at stain after stain.

"You see, right there . . . and there . . . and there. These are the stains I'm talking about. Can't you see them?" Blotch asked passionately. In fact, he was speaking so loudly that he was starting to draw attention from neighbors in the village.

That's when his friend finally looked him in the eye. "Keep your voice down, and listen to me, Blotch." Slowly and clearly the man said, "There . . . are . . . no . . . stains."

Suddenly, Blotch understood. His friends knew there were stains. Everyone in this town knew there were stains. But they had all decided to pretend the stains weren't there.

Everyone in Pretendtown had just decided to ignore the stains. They didn't like them, they didn't want them, but they didn't know what to do with them. Instead of looking for a solution, they chose to pretend the problem didn't even exist.

Blotch finally fell asleep that night, sad for his new friends and the other people of Pretendtown.

Chapter 4
The Pointers

Blotch woke early the next morning before his friends or anyone else in Pretendtown was awake. He was eager to continue his journey and find an answer to the problem of the stains. As he rolled up his sleeping bag and packed his backpack, he thought about the people he had met so far and shook his head. *I wonder if anyone, anywhere, knows how we could ever get rid of our stains. Surely the King can help me.*

As he walked down the road that early morning, Blotch thought about his mother, father, and brothers. He imagined how wonderful it would be if he found the answer to the stains. He daydreamed of what a happy day his family could have if each one of them were finally clean.

But Blotch had found no answers on his journey, and the people he had met so far only made him worry he might never find answers. But this was no time to give up because just ahead was another village. Maybe someone there could point him in the right direction.

Long before Blotch made it to the village, he could tell this was no ordinary place. From a distance he could see that the village was divided by a wide street running all the way through town. Even though the street was wide and open, there was no one on the street. But there were lots of busy people on either side of it.

Reaching the edge of town, Blotch was walking right down the center of that wide-open street when he heard a voice from the left side of the road. "What are you doing out there? Get over here, quick!"

Blotch looked to his left and saw that the voice came from a young man who had more stains than even the people of Pretendtown! But Blotch walked over to the side of the street just as he was instructed.

"I . . . I'm sorry," Blotch said to the young man. "Is it wrong to walk on the street in this town?"

"Well, there's nothing wrong with walking on the street, but I wouldn't do it," the young man said. "It's just not safe."

"Not safe?" repeated Blotch. That was all he needed to hear. "Well, I won't be here long then. I'm just on a journey to see if anyone knows how to get rid of our stains."

The young man narrowed his eyes and looked right at Blotch. "Getting rid of our stains, eh? I don't know about that, but I do know where they come from. . . ." He snarled his lip and pointed to the other side of the street. "From those people over there!"

Just then a new stain appeared on his pointing hand.

"See, I told you," he said, nodding at the new stain. "Welcome to Point City."

One person giving stains to another person didn't sound right to Blotch, but he decided to follow this new friend back to his neighborhood, just in case.

The young man started to explain, "For a long time we didn't know where the stains came from until one day we realized the people on the other side of the road were giving them to us. Can you believe that?"

"That actually is pretty hard to believe," said Blotch. "I thought our stains came from the things we did wrong. Even if other people could give us stains, why would they?"

"I have no idea, my friend, but those people are sneaky, and they are good at staining us. Every time I think about it, I just want to punch someone in the nose!" As he finished his sentence, another giant mark appeared on his arm, right in front of both of them.

"See? You see? They did it again!" he cried. He pointed across the street and screamed at nobody in particular, "It's all your fault!"

Blotch stared wide-eyed at his new friend. After the young man had calmed down a bit, Blotch began, "Have you ever thought that . . . well, that maybe you might be . . . wrong?" Blotch watched the young man's face redden again. Blotch spoke more quickly now. "See, I don't think the people across the street are causing your stains. I don't think they could put stains on you even if they wanted to."

The young man looked at Blotch with big eyes but didn't say a word, so Blotch continued. "I believe our stains don't come from someone else—they come from us."

Blotch watched as several new stains appeared over the man's face and neck.

"You're one of them!" he finally shouted. "I can't believe I brought you over here. You're one of them!" He was jumping up and down and pointing at Blotch. People from all over his side of the street started running toward Blotch and pointing too.

"He's one of them!" they joined in.

Everywhere Blotch looked, people were running at him, snarling, shouting, and pointing their fingers. He didn't know what to do, so he ran in a panic to the other side of the street.

Blotch hoped that the people on the other side of the street might be nicer, might protect him from the mob he just left behind. But as soon as he crossed the street, the people from the other side started pointing and shouting and calling him a "stain thrower."

They were just like the people he was running from!

Blotch didn't know where to go, so he ran back to the center of the road while people from both sides stood on the edges and pointed at him, blaming him for stains that were their own fault.

Without looking back, Blotch ran away from Point City as fast as he could.

Chapter 5
The King

Blotch ran and ran and ran. His legs were sorer than they were after a day of cutting firewood with his father. He was more out of breath than the day his oldest brother teased him by pushing him under the water at the lake. He ran until he could run no longer.

Blotch was too afraid to turn around and look, but he ran far enough and fast enough to know that the finger-pointing people of Point City were no longer behind him. After the longest run of his life, little Blotch finally came to a stop in the middle of the road.

As he caught his breath, he thought about all he had seen and heard on his journey.

He thought about the unfriendly people of Hiderville who lived in fear of their secret truths being uncovered.

He thought of the nice people of Pretendtown, and he knew that ignoring their stains didn't solve the problem.

And how could he forget the people of Point City? They were angry, divided, and fighting while they tried to convince themselves that their stains were someone else's fault.

Blotch was so tired and confused that he started to cry right there where he had stopped. He cried so hard that his eyes blurred and the little bit of strength left in his legs gave way. He dropped to his knees, right in the middle of the road.

Although he had his face in his hands and his knees in the dirt, he could feel the sun's warmth fading. Far from any village and out of food, still stained with no answers, little Blotch was just about to give up.

That's when he felt a hand on his shoulder—a hand as gentle as his mother's but still firm like his father's. Then he heard a man's friendly voice call him by name. "There, there, my little Blotch," it said. "You have had a long journey, and the road has been difficult. Come, follow me."

The voice was so comforting that Blotch thought of nothing but obeying. He somehow found the strength to rise to his feet and follow.

The kind man led Blotch to a little house not far from the side of the road. Once inside he invited the young journeyer to have a seat. The house was small and simple but tidy inside. Although Blotch had never been to the house before and did not know the man, he felt oddly comfortable and perfectly safe.

This new stranger sat across from Blotch. "You can stop crying now. All is well. There's no more need to run. Here you can lay down your hurts, fears, and mistakes. Here you will find rest."

4.4

Blotch's eyes were still blurry from crying, so he squeezed them shut and opened them wide again to try to see this new friend more clearly. The first thing Blotch could make out was the man's amazing smile. The smile invited him to speak.

"I have been on a long journey, looking for answers, and I have found nothing," Blotch began.

"Really?" the man replied. It sounded like a question, but Blotch was almost certain the man already knew who he was and what he was doing on his journey. Still, the voice asked, "What have you been seeking on your journey?"

"I have been trying to find out how to get rid of these stains," Blotch answered.

"Very interesting. Have you found anyone who can help you?"

"I found some people who covered up their stains only to have them revealed. I found others who pretended they had no stains, but on the inside they knew. And I found a group who tried to blame everyone else for their own stains. That's who I was running from," Blotch said desperately. "So, I guess the answer is no. I have found no one to take away the stains."

"Well, little Blotch, do you know where the stains come from?" the man asked. Yet again, it seemed as though he already knew the answer.

"I think I do," Blotch said. "The stains come from us. They appear when we do something wrong, something that deserves a stain. Oh, how I wish we could get rid of them."

The kind man's smile widened even more. "Oh, little Blotch! I have good news: I can take your stains away."

Blotch's eyes cleared enough for him to see the kind man well for the first time. It was the King of the entire kingdom—and he had no stains!

"You . . . you're the King!" Blotch shouted. He shook his head in disbelief. "You can really take away my stains?"

"First things first, little one. I have come to live on this road to help stained ones like you," he said. "I have watched you, all of you, since the beginning of time. I've waited for you to understand that the stains were yours, that you needed someone else to clean them for you."

Blotch interrupted, "But, you're the King. Shouldn't you be living in a castle far away?"

The King laughed and pulled Blotch into a hug.

"Oh, I could do that my child, but I love you and all my people so much that I wanted to be here with you, to take away your stains."

Blotch's heart began to race, even faster than when he was running on the road. "Oh, please, please take away my stains. I am sorry for all the things I've done to cause them. I can't think of anything better than for you to take my stains away."

Blotch fell to his knees at the King's feet. He felt something more powerful than curiosity, something stronger than hope. He had belief! He believed—he knew—that the King had the power to take away his stains.

The King placed a gentle hand on Blotch's shoulder. "Close your eyes," the King whispered.

Blotch immediately obeyed, waiting for what the King would do or say next.

"Your faith has healed you, young Blotch. Now look," the King said.

Blotch opened his eyes and immediately looked down at his own arms, his hands, his feet—the stains were gone! Completely gone!

He ran to a mirror and touched his perfect skin—not one spot, not one blemish looked back at him.

"But how?! Where did they go?" he said, turning toward the King. Suddenly, Blotch jumped back in shock; the King was now covered in stains.

"How can this be? How could this happen? If you can heal me, can you not heal yourself?"

Blotch continued to ask questions, but the King said not a word. He simply waited for Blotch to understand. When little Blotch looked more closely, he recognized the stains upon the King.

They were his. The stains that had once been on Blotch's arms and face and feet were now on the King.

The King then spoke with the same gentle strength, "The stains were yours, but I was willing to take them for you. I have taken your stains because I care for you so much."

Little Blotch began to cry once again, this time not because he was tired or sad. This time he cried because he had never felt so loved.

"Go home, little Blotch, and show your family what has been done. Tell them the good news, and bring them here to me," said the King. "I love them as well, and I will make them clean."

And that is what Blotch planned to do. But he would tell more than his family; he would tell everyone he met what the King had done for him!

Quickly, Blotch gathered his things and headed toward the road to start the long journey home. A few steps from the house, he turned to see his King one more time. Blotch was surprised once more. The King was standing in the middle of the road smiling and waving, and the stains He had taken from Blotch . . . were completely gone!

What an amazing King!

On the way home, Blotch stopped to tell the Pointers in Point City the good news. He tried to convince the Pretenders of Pretendtown to go to the King. And he whispered the good news to the Hiders in Hiderville.

Not all believed, and not all would listen. But many did. And many found themselves walking that same road to the King.

Everyone who came to the King found healing. Their stains were finally gone.

Family Discussion Guide

The story of Blotch is a great tool for creating discussion about God, Jesus, and personal salvation.

I suggest you read the entire story on your own and review the discussion guides before reading the story with your child.

- Day 1—Read chapter 1 and use discussion guide 1.
- Day 2—Read chapter 2 and use discussion guide 2.
- Day 3—Read chapter 3 and use discussion guide 3.
- Day 4—Read chapter 4 and use discussion guide 4.
- Day 5—Read chapter 5 and use discussion guide 5.

Use "A Parent's Guide for Leading a Child to Christ" on page 63 at any point in the process.

CHAPTER 1 DISCUSSION GUIDE
The Journey Begins

Sin is a word that means "to miss the mark." Take turns throwing crumpled pieces of paper into a small trashcan. When someone makes the basket, everyone can yell "Hit!" But when someone misses, sadly say "miss." Explain that the word *sin* simply means missing the target of what God has for us. That is why everyone has sinned.

Questions to discuss with your children:

1. *How did Blotch and the other people get their stains?*

2. *You and I don't have spots appearing on our bodies, but in what way do we have the same problems that Blotch does?*

3. *Romans 3:23 says, "For all have sinned and fall short of the glory of God." How does this verse show that everybody has sinned?*

4. *What is sin? (Affirm your children and explain sin using the illustration at the top of this page.)*

5. *Why do you think Blotch wanted to get rid of his stains so badly?*

6. *Do you think we should try to get rid of our sins? How should we do it?*

7. *Blotch is looking for the King to get rid of his stains. Who should we go to if we want our sins forgiven?*

CHAPTER 2 DISCUSSION GUIDE
The Hiders

Find an envelope, and seal a love note, piece of candy, or gift card inside for each child. Then ask the children to guess what is inside the envelope. After several guesses, let them open the envelope and receive their gift (one per child). Be prepared to share later that some things can only be made good when they are no longer hidden.

Questions to discuss with your children:

1. *How did you feel when you opened your envelope?*

2. *The Hiders of Hiderville only covered up their stains. Why does covering up stains really not do any good?*

3. *How do we try to cover up our stains and mistakes?*

4. *Even if we hide our mistakes from others, who will always know? Why does that matter?*

5. *Proverbs 28:13 says, "The one who conceals his sins will not prosper, but whoever confesses and renounces them will find mercy." What does the word* prosper *mean? What would have happened to the gift in your envelope if you had never opened it?*

6. *How can hiding mistakes keep us from getting rid of our stains?*

CHAPTER 3 DISCUSSION GUIDE
The Pretenders

We can learn about confession by practicing it. Model confession to your children by sharing something you regret or did wrong. Then ask them to share something they have done wrong and regret. Be prepared to compare this experience to confessing and being honest with yourself and God.

Questions to discuss with your children:

1. *Why do you think some people try to ignore their mistakes and pretend they haven't messed up?*

2. *Why does ignoring a mistake, like the Pretenders did, never make it go away?*

3. *First John 1:8–9 says, "If we say, 'We have no sin,' we are deceiving ourselves, and the truth is not in us. If we confess our sins, He is faithful and righteous to forgive us our sins and to cleanse us from all unrighteousness." According to these verses, is there anything you could confess that God would not forgive?*

4. *Blotch wasn't satisfied to pretend his stains were gone—he wanted to be clean. What does 1 John 1:8–9 tell us to do if we want to be clean too?*

5. *Why is it important to confess (tell God about our mistakes)?*

CHAPTER 4 DISCUSSION GUIDE
The Pointers

Gather the family, and explain that you have candy for everyone to enjoy. But when you give out the candy, make sure you are one piece short. Begin to blame different family members for taking the lost piece of candy. Finally, reveal that you had the lost piece all along. Talk about how it feels to be blamed and to blame others.

Questions to discuss with your children:

1. *When has someone blamed you for something that wasn't your fault?*

2. *Have you ever wanted to blame someone to get out of trouble? Why?*

3. *Why will the Pointers never lose their stains if they keep acting like they do?*

4. *Matthew 7:2–5 says, "For with the judgment you use, you will be judged, and with the measure you use, it will be measured to you. Why do you look at the speck in your brother's eye but don't notice the log in your own eye? Or how can you say to your brother, 'Let me take the speck out of your eye,' and look, there's a log in your eye? Hypocrite! First take the log out of your eye, and then you will see clearly to take the speck out of your brother's eye."*

Why do you think it's easier to point at someone else's mistakes than to point at your own?

5. God's Word says that we can't measure our lives by anyone else's life. Why does He want us to focus on our own lives?

6. God doesn't want you to be a Pointer. Is there anything in your life that you want to be honest with God about?

CHAPTER 5 DISCUSSION GUIDE
The King

Ask your children what their favorite toy or possession is, and if possible let them show it to you. Discuss why that toy is so valuable to them, and then share an object or keepsake that is very valuable to you. Finally, ask the kids what it would take for them to give their treasure away to anyone who wanted it. Use this discussion later when discussing what God gave us in Jesus.

Questions to discuss with your children:

1. How did you feel when Blotch met the King?

2. Were you sad when Blotch's stains appeared on the King? Why?

3. John 3:16 tells us, "For God loved the world in this way: He gave His One and Only Son, so that everyone who believes in Him will not perish but have eternal life." According to this verse, how much does God love us?

4. Blotch went on a long journey to get his stains removed. What does John 3:16 tell us that we need to do?

5. The King in this story is like Jesus from the Bible. Would you be willing to let Jesus take away your sins?

A PARENT'S GUIDE FOR LEADING A CHILD TO CHRIST

1. Pray for the child. Let the child hear you pray.

2. Talk about Blotch, and see if the child can identify with him in the story.

3. Share the story of Jesus:

    - We were lost and hopeless.

    - God loved us and sent His Son.

    - Jesus took the punishment that our sins deserved.

    - We can be forgiven if we let Jesus take our place.

    - We need to live our lives for Him.

4. If the child understands and desires to ask Christ into his life, lead him in this simple prayer. Pause after reading each phrase to allow your child to pray it aloud:

Dear God,
Please forgive me for my sins.
Thank You for loving me.
Thank You for sending Jesus for me.

Thank You, Jesus, for dying on the cross for me.
Thank You, Jesus, for rising from the grave for me.
I will live my life for You.
I ask You to be my Lord and Savior.
In Jesus' name I pray, amen.

IMPORTANT FOLLOW-UP ITEMS

- Ask your child to share his or her decision with a friend or family member immediately.
- Celebrate this time! One option is to purchase a new Bible and write the date in it so your child always remembers this day.
- Together with your child, talk to your church about baptism.
- Help your child's faith grow by reading the Bible together, praying together, and talking about God on a daily basis.

Thank you for caring about children and serving the Lord!